Nostalgic Short Stories for Seniors

Heartwarming Tales that Stimulate Nostalgia and Engagement – Memory Prompts After Each Story to Promote Discussion and Activity

Lillian Whitmore

Your Free Gift

As a thank you for your purchase, here is a free copy of **101 Powerful Memory Prompts and Conversation Starters**. This supplementary resource is perfect for reliving cherished memories and can be used digitally or as a printable activity template.

If you cannot scan the QR code below, you can download the PDF at **www.seniorshortstories.com/thank-you**.

Contents

Introduction   IX

1. The First Vinyl Record   1

2. Ice Cream Custard   4

3. The Joy of Mud   7

4. Lightning Bugs   10

5. The Final Clue   13

6. The Best Seat in the House   16

7. The Accidental Chef   19

8. Friday Nights at the Roller Rink   22

9. Sick Day with Grandpa   25

10. Great Heights with Aunt Nora   28

11. Fresh Bread and Amore   32

12. My Disaster with Bangs   35

13. Weekend Adventures at the Lake   38

14. Grandma's Surprises   41

15. The Zamboni   44

16. Perfume and Pioneers   47

17. Flashlight Tag   50

18. My First Job   53

19. The Gift of Gymnastics   56

20. Grandma's Kitchen and the Throne   59

21. Christmas Morning Traditions   62

22. Waffles and Sausages   65

23. Sunday Dinner   68

24. Walks on the Pier   71

25. Polaroid Moments   74

26. Swinging into Friendship   77

27. Casper's Great Rescue   80

28. The Mistletoe Mission   83

29. Summer Nights at the Drive-In   86

30. School Night Birthday   89

31. The Great Coaster Battle   92

32. Saturday Mornings at Denny's   95

33. Ice Cream Truck Jingle   98

34. Best Dentist Trip Ever   101

35. Passover Delight   104

36. My 70s Toys   107

37. Mini Bikes   110

38. Days at the Ballpark   112

Passing the Magic Along   115

Introduction

When I was a kid, I loved spending time with my grandma. During the summers, my mom would drop me off at her house in the mornings, and I would spend all day there until she picked me up after work. We would make food and watch shows together—her favorites were Wheel of Fortune and Jeopardy. But my favorite activity was reading books out loud with her. She believed it helped me with pronunciation and public speaking (often making me reread sentences to express emotions and intentions correctly). It also helped keep her mind sharp by exposing her to topics she might not have chosen.

She introduced me to Nancy Drew, her favorite series growing up, and I introduced her to Redwall, my favorite series. Right after reading a chapter, we always paused and discussed new concepts, character's actions, places, etc. If we hit an exciting topic, we would go on a tangent and look up other books to learn more. Reading sparked countless conversations between my grandmother and me, and I truly cherished those moments.

These memories inspire this series. **The stories in this book are inspired by readers who have been asked to share a memory from childhood that makes them feel nostalgic for the good ol' days.**

I hope these stories spark memories, joy, or curiosity. If you're reading this with a friend or a group, I hope the conversation starters will evoke memories and strengthen bonds through the timeless power of storytelling.

Chapter 1

The First Vinyl Record

My entire world revolved around a small record shop on Oak Elm Street when I was ten. Music had always been a part of my life, mainly from the radio or from the records my sister Linda played over and over again. But I wanted something of my own that would speak to me in a way no one else could understand.

One Saturday, I wandered into the record shop for the first time. The warm, musty scent of vinyl washed over me the moment I stepped inside, mingling with a catchy tune that played softly in the background. As I browsed through the rows of records, my eyes landed on a simple yet striking cover: a young man holding a cat, sitting beside a woman in red. It was Bob Dylan's *Bringing It All Back Home*.

My heart skipped a beat. I'd heard Dylan's gritty, poetic voice on the radio before, and something about it resonated with me like no other music had. I knew in that instant that I needed that record. But when I looked at the price tag—$4.99—it felt like an impossible dream. My weekly allowance was just 50 cents, and it would take me ten long weeks of saving every penny to afford it.

But I was determined. I resisted the usual temptations of candy and comic books and started mowing lawns, running errands, and even helping old Mrs. Jenkins with her gardening for extra coins. I'd visit the record shop each week to ensure the album was still there. The shopkeeper, Mr. Hendricks, began to recognize me and always greeted me with a knowing smile. "Still here, son. It's waiting for you," he'd say, and I'd nod, feeling that little flutter of hope every time.

Finally, after what felt like an eternity, I had saved exactly five dollars. My heart pounded as I walked to the record shop, clutching my hard-earned money. Mr. Hendricks greeted me warmly, and I could tell he understood what this day meant to me. After paying, I clutched the brown paper bag with the record inside and raced home, feeling like I was holding a piece of the world in my hands.

"What's got you in such a hurry?" my mom asked as I burst through the door, breathless and grinning from ear to ear.

"I got it, Mom!" I exclaimed, holding up the bag triumphantly.

She smiled at me, understanding my excitement even if she didn't quite share it. "Well, go on then. Let's hear it."

I rushed to the living room, carefully placing the record on the family's turntable. My hands shook slightly as I lowered the needle onto the vinyl, and then, as it touched down, the room filled with Bob Dylan's raw, honest voice. I closed my eyes, letting the music wash over me. It was as if the songs were speaking directly to me, offering a glimpse into a world beyond the borders of our small town.

When the last notes finally faded, I opened my eyes and smiled. The world still felt vast and full of promise, but now I had a soundtrack to go with it. This record, this music, was mine. And I knew it would be the first of many.

Memory Prompts

- Describe the first time you ever purchased a record. Who was the artist, and why did you want that record?

- Do you remember the first song you ever learned the lyrics to?

- Did you have a favorite shop you visited growing up?

Chapter 2

Ice Cream Custard

When I was a little girl, barely old enough to understand the world around me, my family lived with my maternal grandparents on their farm while my dad served in Korea. Those days were filled with the simple joys of country life, surrounded by fields, animals, and the rhythms of a farm that provided everything we needed.

We ate well—fresh vegetables from the garden, eggs from the chickens, and meat from animals my grandparents raised themselves. But some things were considered special, "store-bought" treats that we rarely had.

One of my earliest memories is of trips to town with my mom and Grandma. My two younger brothers and I were too little to go inside the stores, so we would wait in the car, our legs dangling from the seats, eyes wide with anticipation. The reward for our patience was simple but glorious—a package of hot dogs and a bag of buns.

We'd tear into them once we got home, savoring every bite as if it were the most gourmet meal in the world. But as good as those hot dogs were, there was one treat we never got from the store: ice cream.

Store-bought ice cream was a luxury we couldn't afford, but Grandma had a way of making up for it. And it's that memory, more than any other, that has stayed with me all these years.

Grandma didn't have an ice cream churn, at least not one I ever saw, but she made the most delicious ice cream in the world. She would start by cooking up a custard. I don't remember what went into it—just that it was creamy, sweet, and made with love. After the custard was done, she would pour it into a rectangular cake pan and carefully place it in the freezer. Hours would pass, and we'd wait in eager anticipation.

When the time finally came, Grandma would take the pan out and set it on the counter. She used a big butcher knife to pry pieces of the frozen custard out of the pan. It was unlike anything you could buy in a store.

I can still picture that dining room, with its thin curtains drawn against the afternoon sun and an old black metal fan slowly stirring the warm air. My brothers and I would gather around the table, our eyes wide as Grandma handed out chunks of homemade ice cream. We gave my baby brother Mark his first bite of ice cream, his little face lighting up with shock, then delight.

I couldn't have been older than four, but that moment is as clear to me as if it happened yesterday.

Memory Prompts

- Was there something in your child that was considered a "store-bought treat"?

- Do you remember the first time you ever had ice cream? What flavor was it?

- Describe your perfect ice cream dessert. What toppings would you put on it? Would it be in a cone?

Chapter 3

The Joy of Mud

One of the fondest memories I have from my childhood isn't tied to any vacation or cool toy. Instead, it's wrapped up in the simple, messy joy of playing in the mud. Something about those afternoons behind our garage stays with me even now.

My mom was an avid gardener, and most of our yard was filled with her beautiful flowers. The colors bloomed in every corner, and she tended to them with the kind of love and care that only a gardener knows. But behind the garage was a different kind of paradise—our little mud kingdom.

Mom knew that kids needed a place to dig, explore, and get dirty, so she designated that spot for us. It was the one area where we could dig holes, mix in water, and create the biggest, sloppiest batches of mud. The only rule was simple: we had to fill the hole back in when we were done. It was our responsibility, and we took it seriously, mostly because we knew our precious mud pit might disappear if we didn't.

After a particularly heavy rain one summer day, our mud hole became a sloshy swamp. The rainwater had filled the hole to the brim, creating a glorious, squishy, three or four feet of thick mud. It was irresistible.

My little brother, always daring, was the first to test the waters—or rather, the mud. He jumped in with both feet, sinking down with a squelch. We laughed so hard as he tried to move, but the mud clung to him like it had a mind of its own. He squealed in delight, his voice echoing around the yard as he tried to pull himself out.

The noise must have carried into the house because soon enough, Mom came out to see what all the commotion was about. She took one look at my brother, stuck in the mud, and shook her head with a knowing smile. "Alright, get him out," she said, but the mud had other plans. When we finally managed to pull him free, his shoes stayed behind, buried deep in the muck.

"Go get his shoes," Mom ordered, and we groaned, knowing there was only one way to retrieve them—by going in headfirst. We ended up covered from head to toe, but we got the shoes back, and the adventure made it all worth it.

Another time, the neighbors behind us were putting in a swimming pool. The tractor operator was digging up a mountain of dirt, and we couldn't help but ask if he could dump some of it over our fence. He said he would if our mom agreed, and when she gave the nod, we were in heaven. That pile of dirt, four or five feet high, became the foundation for the best mud we ever made.

After hours of play, Mom would meet us on the back patio when it was time to go inside. She would hose us off, the cold water washing away the mud and the evidence of our day's fun. She'd laugh as we squirmed and shrieked, and once we were somewhat clean, she'd have a warm bath ready for us inside.

Those afternoons spent playing in the mud were more than just fun—they were about the joy of getting dirty and the love of a mom who understood the importance of letting kids be kids.

Memory Prompts

- Did you like playing in the dirt or mud growing up? If so, describe what you liked to do.

- Describe the place that you grew up in. Did you have a yard or play in a nearby park?

- Do you think kids nowadays play outside as much as you did growing up?

Chapter 4

Lightning Bugs

When I was growing up, it was a tradition in our family to gather outside once dusk came around. My sisters and I would run barefoot across the lawn, our laughter filling the air as we chased each other and waited for the first flicker of a lightning bug. It was as if the tiny, glowing creatures knew just when to appear, their lights blinking on and off, signaling that the night's adventures were about to begin.

Mom would always bring out a big bowl of popcorn, the salty, buttery aroma wafting through the air, mingling with the scent of freshly cut grass. She'd set it on the porch, and we'd all dig in, our fingers slick with butter as we reached for more.

Kool-Aid was our drink of choice—usually cherry or grape—and we sipped it happily from plastic cups, leaving bright-colored stains on our lips. Meanwhile, Mom and Dad would sit on the porch steps, nursing a couple of beers, their faces relaxed and content as they watched us play.

The best part of those evenings was catching lightning bugs. My dad would help my sisters and me poke holes in the tops of old pickle jars, the kind with the ridged glass. We'd run around, jars in hand, carefully capturing the little glowing bugs, mesmerized by their gentle light. The whole family would join in, and neighbors walking by would wave and laugh as they watched us dart across the lawn.

"I got one!" my little sister would shout, her voice full of excitement as she peered into her jar, watching the tiny creature light up. Dad would help her screw the lid on, making sure the holes were just big enough for air but not big enough for escape.

As the night wore on, we gathered on the porch, comparing our jars and counting the lightning bugs we had caught. Mom and Dad talked with the neighbors who had stopped by, everyone enjoying the simplicity of the evening.

When it was time for bed, we'd insist on bringing our jars inside, eager to keep our glowing treasures close. Dad would always say it was okay, even though I'm sure it was a hassle to lug those jars into the house. We'd place them on our nightstands, the soft light casting a gentle glow in our dark rooms. It was like having a piece of the summer night with us as we drifted off to sleep.

But by morning, without fail, the jars would be empty. The lightning bugs were gone, and we'd shrug it off, assuming they had somehow slipped through the tiny holes in the lid. We didn't know that after we fell asleep, Dad would sneak into our rooms, carefully take the jars outside, and release the bugs back into the night. Then, like magic, he'd return the empty jars to their places, leaving us to wonder how the bugs had "gotten away."

Memory Prompts

- Have you ever seen lightning bugs?

- Did you have any other bugs that you saw a lot of in your yard or neighborhood?

- Is there any bug you are afraid of or do not like seeing?

Chapter 5

The Final Clue

Growing up with a brother who was twelve years older than me was like having a mix between a sibling and a superhero. He was the one who protected me, made me laugh, and, most memorably, turned ordinary days into extraordinary adventures.

One of my favorite memories from childhood was when he would set up scavenger hunts around the house for me. They weren't just any scavenger hunts—they were filled with clever clues that led me from one spot to the next, each one a little riddle that my young mind would puzzle over with delight.

Each hunt always ended the same way: with a Hostess cupcake in the microwave. It became our little tradition. I still remember the thrill of opening the microwave door, knowing that my "treasure" awaited me.

As I grew older, the scavenger hunts became less frequent. Life got busier—school, friends, and all the other things that come with growing up. My brother was always there, but the hunts were something that faded into the background as childhood gave way to adolescence.

The time I graduated from high school was a big moment that was exciting and a little scary as I thought about what lay ahead. Amid all the celebrations, I found myself reminiscing about those scavenger hunts from years ago. One day, I casually mentioned it to my brother, telling him how much those little adventures had meant to me.

As I was getting ready on the morning of my graduation, I noticed a small envelope on my dresser with my name on it. Inside was a note: "The adventure isn't over yet. Start in the kitchen."

My heart skipped a beat as I realized what was happening. I rushed to the kitchen, where I found the first clue taped to the refrigerator. It was just like old times, except now the riddles were a little more challenging.

Each clue led me to a different part of the house—the living room, the backyard, and even the garage. My excitement grew with each discovery, a wave of nostalgia washing over me as I remembered the joy of those childhood hunts.

Finally, the last clue led me to the microwave. I couldn't help but smile as I opened the door, half-expecting to find a cupcake waiting for me. But this time, it was something different. Inside was an envelope, and when I opened it, I found two tickets to The Summer Jam with a note that read, "Congratulations, bud. Proud of you."

The Summer Jam was incredible, but it wasn't just about the music or the incredible crowds. It was about sharing that experience with him. My brother is the best I could ever ask for, and those scavenger hunts—both then and now—are just one of the many reasons why. I think I'll go get a Hostess cupcake now.

Memory Prompts

- Describe your favorite concert you've ever been to.

- Have you ever done a scavenger hunt? Or maybe even an Easter Egg hunt?

- If you could do a scavenger hunt like the one in the story, what snack would you like to find as a prize?

Chapter 6

The Best Seat in the House

Growing up, my parents were masters at turning the ordinary into something extraordinary. We didn't have much, but they never let that stop them from making life feel special. They made us feel like we were the luckiest kids in the world, even when money was tight. One of the best examples was when they turned our living room into the best baseball experience I've ever had.

Baseball was a big deal in our house. We loved watching the games on TV, cheering for our favorite teams, and dreaming about the day we'd finally get to see a game in person. I remember talking about it all the time—how incredible it would be to sit in the stands, feel the energy of the crowd, and maybe even catch a foul ball. But as much as I wanted to go, I knew we couldn't afford it.

I had pretty much accepted that our baseball dreams would stay within the confines of our TV set until one unforgettable day.

It was a regular school day, or so I thought. When my siblings and I got home, we were met with a surprise that blew our minds. There, on the kitchen table, were tickets to that night's game! I couldn't believe my eyes. My mom had created them herself, each one with our names on it, and she even made fake money for us to "spend" at the game.

"Better go get cleaned up," Mom said, a twinkle in her eye. "You don't want to be late for the game!"

We couldn't get ready fast enough. When we came back, our living room had been transformed. Chairs were arranged in rows, each one numbered to match the seat numbers on our tickets. My dad stood at the doorway, playing the role of the ticket taker.

"Welcome to the ballpark!" he said, a big grin on his face as he tore our tickets in half and handed them back to us. "You're in section A, row 2, seat 3. Enjoy the game!"

We giggled as we found our seats, the anticipation building. My mom had even thought of dimming the lights and turning up the volume on the TV, making the game feel larger than life. As the first pitch was thrown, we were already on the edge of our seats, fully immersed in the experience.

But the best part was yet to come. My parents disappeared into the kitchen a few innings in, only to emerge with a tray of hot dogs, candy, and soda. "Hot dogs! Get your hot dogs!" they called out, just like vendors at a real game.

We scrambled to pull out the fake money Mom had given us and eagerly bought our snacks, feeling like we were really at the ballpark. We laughed, cheered, and stuffed ourselves with all the goodies they'd prepared.

I didn't care that we hadn't actually gone to the ballpark. It felt like we had—only better. To this day, I still think of that night as the best baseball game I've ever been to.

Memory Prompts

- Did you or your family enjoy watching baseball together growing up?

- If you were to be part of a re-enactment of a baseball game, what part would you like to be? The ticket taker, the hot dog vendor, an audience member, a baseball player, etc.?

- Describe one of your favorite memories of your parents surprising you.

Chapter 7

The Accidental Chef

One afternoon in fourth grade, I came home from school and found a note waiting for me on the kitchen counter. It was from my mom. The note read, "Hey baby, go ahead and start dinner when you get home, please. The pasta and sauce are on the kitchen counter, and the meat is in the fridge. I love you!"

I couldn't believe it. My mom was trusting me to make dinner! I was nine years old, and while I'd watched my mom, dad, and grandma make spaghetti a million times, I'd never actually done it myself. But I was excited—no, thrilled—that she thought I could handle it. In my mind, I was about to step into the big leagues.

I set to work immediately. I found the meat in the sink, just like she said, and the pasta and sauce were in the fridge. I remembered all the times I'd watched them make dinner: boiling the water, browning the meat, stirring the sauce. It didn't seem that hard. I filled a pot with water, placed it on the stove, and turned on the burner, waiting for it to come to a boil.

While the water heated up, I started on the meat. I dropped it into a pan and used a spatula to break it up, just like I'd seen my mom do countless times. The smell of browning meat filled the kitchen, and I could feel a sense of pride bubbling up inside me. This was going to be good.

Once the water was boiling, I carefully added the pasta, stirring it often like I'd seen my dad do, making sure it didn't stick together. I kept an eye on the meat, ensuring it didn't burn, and then poured the sauce into the pan, mixing everything with a wooden spoon. The kitchen was warm and smelled delicious, and I felt like a real chef.

By the time my parents got home, I was just about finished. I had the spaghetti drained and the sauce ready to go, and I was beaming with pride. But when they walked into the kitchen, I was met with a look of shock on their faces.

"Hey! You made dinner!" my mom exclaimed, her eyes wide.

"Yep!" I said, grinning from ear to ear. "Just like you asked!"

My mom glanced at the note on the counter, then back at me, and suddenly it all made sense to her. "Oh no," she said, half laughing. "That note was for your dad, not you! I didn't think you'd think I meant you!"

She was worried, of course, because I could have hurt myself with the boiling water or while cooking the meat. But after the initial shock wore off, I saw a hint of pride in their eyes. They were surprised—not just that I'd made dinner all by myself, but it had turned out pretty well, too.

We sat down to eat, and I nervously waited for their verdict. But to my delight, they loved it. "This is good," my dad said, and my mom nodded in agreement. "You did a great job."

Over the years, I've perfected my spaghetti recipe, and I like to joke that I have an extra decade of practice on my peers. My parents still laugh about that day. And every time I make spaghetti, I think back to that nine-year-old kid, standing in the kitchen, determined to make dinner just like the grown-ups.

Memory Prompts

- Do you remember the first thing you ever cooked? What was it, and how did it turn out?

- Do you or did you like cooking? If so, describe a few of your signature dishes.

- Do you prefer pasta with white sauce or red sauce?

Chapter 8

Friday Nights at the Roller Rink

My favorite way to spend a Friday night was always at Roller Haven, the small town's buzzing roller skating rink. It was the heart of teenage life, where worries vanished under the glow of disco lights and the beat of the latest tunes.

I could barely contain my excitement as I laced up my white roller skates with bright red wheels, which I had saved for weeks to buy. Every time I slipped them on, I felt like I could fly. The rink was alive with energy, the scent of popcorn and pretzels in the air, mingling with the faint tang of sweat from eager skaters.

"Ready, Grace?" my friend Lisa asked with a playful nudge.

"More than ready," I grinned, adjusting my laces one last time. "Let's go."

We glided onto the smooth wooden floor, joining the steady flow of skaters. The disco ball cast shimmering patterns of light, making everything feel magical. My heart pounded in time with the music—a mix of Bee Gees, Donna Summer, and KC and the Sunshine Band. It was the soundtrack of my life, fueling the joy bubbling inside me.

I loved the atmosphere of the roller rink—the laughter of friends, the excitement of seeing who was there, and the secret hope that a certain someone might notice me.

Halfway through the night, the DJ's voice crackled over the speakers. "Alright, folks, you know what time it is—couples skate! Grab that special someone and get ready for some romance under the disco lights."

My stomach flipped as couples paired up. Lisa and I usually sat out during the couple's skate, giggling from the sidelines, but tonight felt different. Just as I was about to suggest a snack break, I heard a voice behind me.

"Hey, Grace, want to skate?"

I turned around to see Ryan, the boy from my English class who always sat two rows over. Though everyone knew he wasn't the best skater, something about his shy smile always made my heart skip a beat.

"Sure," I replied, a little breathless.

We took to the rink, hand in hand, as the music slowed to a gentle ballad. My nerves faded with each glide, and soon, I was lost in the moment. The lights swirled around us, the music wrapped us in its embrace, and it felt like we were the only two people in the world for those few minutes.

Ryan stumbled a bit, and I laughed. "You okay?" I asked, squeezing his hand.

"Yeah," he chuckled, "just trying to keep up with you."

As the song ended, Ryan smiled at me, and I could feel my cheeks flushing—not just from the skating.

"Thanks, Grace," he said, looking a little bashful. "That was fun."

"It was," I agreed, my heart still racing. "Maybe we can do it again sometime."

"Yeah," Ryan said, his smile widening. "I'd like that."

I couldn't stop smiling as Lisa, and I left the rink that night. The thrill of skating, the music, the lights, and the unexpected moment with Ryan made me feel alive in a way I hadn't before. I couldn't wait to go back next Friday.

Memory Prompts

- Did you ever go to roller rinks when you were growing up?

- Describe one of your favorite activities to do on Friday nights when you were growing up.

- Share one adjective you would use to describe disco music.

Chapter 9

Sick Day with Grandpa

Being the only grandchild for a while had its perks, especially when it came to spending time with Grandpa. He treated me like his little sidekick, and I loved every moment. Whether it was fishing, listening to baseball games on the radio, or just hanging out, Grandpa made me feel like the most important person in the world.

Fishing with Grandpa was always an adventure. He'd take me out on his old boat, where I'd sit behind the wheel and pretend I was the captain, steering us to the best fishing spots. Grandpa would patiently show me how to keep the fish on a stringer and check the pots for crawdads. I wasn't much help, but he never seemed to mind.

When we weren't on the water, we'd sit on his front porch or swing in the backyard, listening to the Kansas City Royals games on the radio. I didn't really understand what was happening in the game, but I pretended I did. Grandpa didn't mind—he just enjoyed having me there beside him. After a while, he'd send me inside to get us a soda. Back then, that meant a tall glass bottle of Pepsi, the kind you had to pop open with a bottle opener. I felt so grown up carrying those bottles back outside.

Sometimes, he'd ask me to grab us an Eskimo Pie. I'd hand one to Grandpa, and we'd eat them together, the chocolate coating cracking with each bite, our fingers sticky by the end.

We played board games occasionally, but Grandpa loved just sitting together, enjoying the day. He wasn't one for a lot of fuss—he just liked to hang out, and his quiet presence comforted me.

One of my most vivid memories is from when I was about 12 or 13. I came down with the worst case of strep throat imaginable. I was bedridden for a week, stuck at home alone while my mom worked her two jobs and my dad was busy with his own. The first day was miserable. I lay there feeling sorry for myself, wishing for someone to take care of me.

Then, on the second day, Grandpa showed up. He brought his little black-and-white TV, the one he usually kept in his own room, and set it up in my bedroom. Suddenly, the day didn't seem so bad. We spent the entire day watching cartoons and game shows. Grandpa even brought along some junk food, the kind my mom never let me have, and a stack of books from the library. I loved reading, but my mom didn't take me to the library often, so this felt like heaven.

He fixed me lunch, washed the dishes, and stayed with me until my brother came home from school. I don't remember much about being sick that week, but I remember how Grandpa made me feel—safe, loved, and not so alone. Those days with Grandpa were some of the best of my childhood, and I'll always be grateful for the time we spent together.

Memory Prompts

- What kind of music or programming did your favorite radio station play when you were growing up?

- When you were sick as a kid, was there a comfort food you wanted to feel better?

- Describe one of your favorite cartoons when you were growing up.

Chapter 10

Great Heights with Aunt Nora

When I was growing up, my cousin Danny and I were inseparable. We spent every waking moment together, plotting adventures and getting into all sorts of mischief. But nothing could have prepared us for the day we convinced my Aunt Nora to ride the roller coaster.

Aunt Nora was a sweet, gentle woman who had a way of making everyone feel loved. She was always baking, tending to her lilacs, or telling us stories about "the good old days." But there was one thing Aunt Nora wasn't—she wasn't adventurous. She was terrified of heights. We knew this because she had told us many times, usually when we tried to get her to join us on the Ferris wheel at the county fair.

"No, no, dears," she'd say, waving us off with a smile. "I'm quite happy with my feet on the ground, thank you very much."

So when Danny and I decided to spend a day at the amusement park that summer, we didn't even think of asking Aunt Nora to come with us, but she surprised us that morning by insisting on joining.

"You're going to need someone to keep an eye on you two rascals," she said, a twinkle in her eye. "And I could use a little fun myself."

Danny and I exchanged excited glances. Having Aunt Nora along would be great—she'd spoil us with cotton candy and other amusement park snacks.

"Let's get Aunt Nora on the roller coaster," he whispered to me as we walked through the gates.

I looked at him like he was crazy. "She's scared of heights! She'll never do it."

Somehow, against all odds, we convinced Aunt Nora that the roller coaster was just a "little ride with a few bumps." She looked at the towering track with some hesitation, but we reassured her that it would be fun.

"Oh, alright," she finally said, clutching her purse a little tighter. "But don't you dare tell me to open my eyes until it's over!"

We promised, crossing our fingers behind our backs.

As the three of us settled into the car, I could see Aunt Nora gripping the safety bar like her life depended on it. Her eyes were squeezed shut before the ride even began. Danny and I exchanged a mischievous grin.

The coaster clanked and clattered as it began its slow ascent to the top. Aunt Nora was mumbling something under her breath—probably a prayer. When we reached the peak, I felt a rush of excitement and panic all at once. The view was spectacular—the entire park was laid out below us. But I knew what was coming next.

Just as the car teetered on the edge of the first big drop, Danny nudged Aunt Nora and whispered, "Okay, Aunt Nora, you can open your eyes now!"

She hesitated for a moment, then cracked one eye open just as we plummeted down the steepest hill. The scream that erupted from her was unlike anything I'd ever heard—half terror, half laughter. Danny and I couldn't stop laughing, even as the wind whipped through our hair and the car careened around sharp turns and dizzying loops.

When the ride finally slowed to a stop, Aunt Nora's face was a mix of relief and exasperation. She looked at us, shaking her head with a smile.

"You boys!" she scolded, though there was no real anger in her voice. "I'll never trust you again!"

But as we walked away, her arm linked with mine, she leaned in and whispered, "That was the most terrifying thing I've ever done. But I'm glad I did it."

Danny and I grinned, knowing we had just shared a moment with Aunt Nora that we would forever remember. And even though she never set foot on a roller coaster again, that summer day became one of her favorite stories to tell—and mine, too.

Memory Prompts

- Did you like going on rollercoasters or fair rides growing up?

- Did your family like to go anywhere during the summers for trips?

- Describe your favorite activity at an amusement park.

Chapter 11

Fresh Bread and Amore

The scent of freshly baked bread filled our kitchen, a warm, comforting aroma that wrapped itself around me like a blanket. I was five years old, perched on the kitchen counter, my tiny legs dangling over the edge. My father, who I adored more than anything, stood beside me, his strong hands gently kneading the dough. Even now, decades later, that memory is so vivid that I can almost smell the bread baking.

It was the early 1970s, and my father, a skilled baker and pastry chef, had always been a man of action. He loved his work, the artistry of creating something beautiful and delicious from simple ingredients. But then, just before my third birthday, he slipped a couple of disks in his back. What was supposed to be a short recovery stretched into three long years, much worse than the doctors had anticipated.

Forced to stay home, my father could no longer work in his beloved bakery. But he found solace in our small kitchen, where he continued to bake, not out of necessity but out of love. Every day, he would lift me up and sit me on the counter, making me his little assistant.

"Ready to make some dough, Alison?" he'd ask, a twinkle in his eye.

I'd nod eagerly, my small hands reaching out to help with the dough. He'd hand me a little piece to play with, and together, we'd knead, shape, and create. The radio would always be on, tuned to his favorite station, where the smooth voice of Dean Martin often crooned in the background.

As soon as the opening notes of "That's Amore" began, my father's face would light up. He'd start to sing along, his deep voice warm and full of affection. And, of course, I'd join in, my childish voice giggling as I tried to keep up with the lyrics.

"When the moon hits your eye, like a big pizza pie, that's amore!" he'd sing, spinning me around in an impromptu kitchen dance.

"That's amore!" I'd echo, my laughter ringing out over the music.

After the bread was shaped and placed in the oven, the kitchen would be filled with the irresistible smell of it baking. We'd sit together, watching the oven door, waiting for the golden crust to form. And then, when the bread was finally ready, we'd break it open and savor that first warm bite, the crusty exterior giving way to the soft, fluffy center.

Those afternoons were followed by quiet evenings on the couch. My father would lie down, and I'd climb onto his chest, snuggling close as we watched old movies. I didn't care much about the plot—what mattered was the comfort of his steady heartbeat beneath my ear and the sound of his voice as he hummed along to the movie's score.

I'd inevitably fall asleep there, lulled by the warmth of his body and the lingering scent of bread in the air. My father would stay still, letting me sleep, even though his back must have ached. It was in those moments that I felt most loved, most secure.

Looking back, I realize that those years of my father's recovery, while difficult in many ways, were also a gift. They gave us time—precious, uninterrupted time—to bond and create memories that would last a lifetime. I learned so much from him, not just about baking but also about patience, resilience, and the importance of finding joy in the little things.

Every time I smell freshly baked bread or hear a Dean Martin song, I'm transported back to that kitchen, to those afternoons with my father. And I can't help but smile, grateful for the love and warmth that filled those days and the memories that remain as rich and comforting as the bread we baked together.

Memory Prompts

- Have you ever had a special activity or routine with a parent or loved one that brought you closer together?

- Have you ever found joy in a small, simple task during a difficult time? What was it, and how did it help you?

- Is there a song or piece of music that instantly takes you back to a specific moment in your life? What memories does it bring up?

Chapter 12

My Disaster with Bangs

I was ten, and I had decided that I was ready for a change. I was tired of the same old hairstyle I'd had for as long as I could remember—long, blonde hair that fell past my shoulders with not a hint of excitement to it. I wanted something bold, something that would make me stand out. And in my youthful wisdom, I figured that giving myself bangs was just the ticket.

Of course, I didn't tell my mom about my plan. She was busy in the garden that afternoon, and I knew she'd never let me cut my hair on my own. But I was determined. Armed with scissors from the kitchen drawer, I locked myself in the bathroom and stood in front of the sink.

The mirror was a bit too high for me to see my full reflection, so I decided to do it without one. After all, how hard could it be? I had seen my mom trim my hair a hundred times—snip, snip, snip, and done. I was confident I could manage it.

With a deep breath, I gathered a section of hair from the front, holding it tightly between my fingers. My heart was racing with a mix of excitement and nerves as I raised the scissors to my hair. I could already picture how fabulous I was going to look with my new bangs.

I made the first cut—straight across, just like I'd seen my mom do. But as the golden strands fell into the sink, my confidence wavered. The section I had cut was a lot shorter than I'd intended. I glanced down at the hair, now about an inch long, lying forlornly in the sink—a knot formed in my stomach.

I tried to fix it, but things only got worse with each snip. My hands were shaking, and the scissors seemed to have a mind of their own. Before I knew it, my once beautiful hair was reduced to a choppy mess, and I knew I was in deep trouble.

My heart sank as I looked at the result. My bangs were uneven and too short, and I looked nothing like the glamorous vision I had imagined. Panic set in, and I did the only thing I could think of—I gathered the cut hair into the waste bin and covered it with a towel, hoping my mom wouldn't notice.

But, of course, she did. As soon as I stepped out of the bathroom, trying to hide my new 'do under a hat, she took one look at me and gasped.

"What did you do?" she asked, her eyes wide with shock.

I burst into tears, unable to hold it in any longer. "I just wanted bangs," I sobbed. "But I messed up!"

She pulled me into a hug, her initial shock melting into sympathy. "Oh, honey, it's okay. It's just hair—it'll grow back."

But even as she comforted me, I could see the glint of amusement in her eyes. She gently lifted the hat off my head, examining the damage. "Well, we'll have to fix this," she said with a smile. "But you're still my beautiful girl, even with these...unique bangs."

We spent the next hour in the bathroom as my mom tried to even out the disaster I had created. In the end, my bangs were much shorter than I had wanted, but they were at least somewhat presentable. And in the waste bin, she found the locks of golden hair I had tried to hide.

To my surprise, instead of throwing them away, she carefully gathered the hair, placing it in a small plastic bag. "One day, you'll look back on this and laugh," she said, tucking the bag in a drawer.

She was right. Years later, whenever I visit my mom, she still has that little bag of hair tucked away, a reminder of my first—and last—attempt at DIY haircuts. And every time we look at it, we laugh, remembering the day I learned that some things are better left to the professionals.

Memory Prompts

- Have you ever made a bold change to your appearance that didn't go as planned? How did you handle it?

- What is a childhood memory that still makes you laugh when you think back on it?

- Did you ever get in trouble for doing something without permission? How did your parents react?

Chapter 13

Weekend Adventures at the Lake

When I was around 11 or 12, Friday afternoons marked the start of a grand adventure. As soon as the final bell rang at school, my friends and I would race home, grab our gear, and load up our bikes with enough food and supplies to last the weekend. We were heading to the lake—a secluded spot nestled on private property, where the river had been dammed to generate electricity. We had permission to camp there, and it was the perfect escape for us.

The ride to the lake was about 3 or 4 kilometers, just far enough to feel like we were leaving the rest of the world behind. Our bikes were heavy with supplies, but the excitement of the weekend ahead made the journey fly by. The path was familiar, winding through fields and past trees that seemed to welcome us back each week.

When we arrived, the first order of business was setting up camp. The shepherd's hut held some of our "extras"—a few old pots, fishing gear, and odds and ends we'd accumulated over time. We'd cut ferns to make soft bedding and stretch a tarp between trees to keep the rain or dew off our heads at night. Once the campsite was ready, we'd get a fire going, the crackling flames promising warmth and a hot meal.

Dinner was simple but satisfying—sausages or something we could quickly cook over the fire. We'd sit around, our bellies full and the firelight flickering on our faces. We'd rise early to fish, casting our lines into the lake's still waters as the morning mist curled off the surface. Rainbow trout were our prize, and there was nothing like the thrill of feeling a tug on the line, the fight to reel it in, and the pride of showing off our catch to the others.

Midday was for lazy activities—relaxing by the lake, collecting fallen branches for firewood, and searching for worms and grubs to use as bait. We knew just where to look—under the acacia trees, where the soil was soft and rich, and along the edges of the lake, where the ground was damp and teeming with life. When the sun was at its peak, we'd retreat to the shade, dozing off with the sounds of nature all around us.

As evening approached, we'd fish again, the setting sun casting a golden glow over the water. The air was cooler, the world quieter, and it felt like time slowed down just for us. The fire would be lit again, and we'd sit around, sharing stories and jokes. Those weekends at the lake were moments of pure freedom. We had no schedules, no worries. We were explorers, fishermen, and best friends, living for the simple pleasures of the outdoors.

Memory Prompts

- Did you and your friends ever go camping or hang out by a certain spot? If so, describe one of your memories.

- What time did you get out of school growing up? What did you like to do after class got out?

Chapter 14

Grandma's Surprises

Spending weekends with my grandmother in the 1960s was like stepping into a world of wonder and love, where every corner of her home held something new and fascinating.

I always got to sleep with her, and there was something so comforting about snuggling up next to her at night. I'd drift off to sleep, listening to the sounds of the old house. In the mornings, I'd wake to the sight of her wringer washing machine, an odd contraption that I was endlessly fascinated by. I watched in awe as she fed clothes through the rollers, amazed at how it squeezed out every last drop of water.

She used an old iron that had to be heated on the stove, and I'd watch, mesmerized, as she pressed her pretty floral handkerchiefs. One day, seeing my curiosity, she handed me the iron and let me try. I carefully smoothed out the fabric, the warm iron gliding over the handkerchiefs, feeling so grown-up and trusted.

Her house was a treasure trove of memories. She still had the dolls that had belonged to my mother and her sisters and hundreds of old paper dolls that I loved playing with. Each one seemed to tell a story, and I'd spend hours dressing them up, imagining their lives in their paper world.

Many weekends, there were new kittens in the barn, and Grandma would teach me how to handle them gently, reminding me not to open their eyes too soon. We'd laugh as they wriggled in our hands, their tiny bodies warm and soft. Her old hound dog, Judy, was always nearby, sleeping on the stairs landing, and he'd be waiting for us every morning, ready to follow us out to the chicken coop to collect eggs for breakfast.

Grandma was the first person to introduce me to grapefruit, and though its tartness was a shock at first, I grew to love it because she loved it. But it was her raspberry pies that I adored most. She was the only one in the family who made them, and to this day, the taste of raspberry pie brings me back to her kitchen, where the scent of baking mingled with the sweet smell of geraniums from the small table by the window.

I still love the smell of geraniums, and every time I catch a whiff of their distinctive scent, I'm transported back to those weekends with her.

Sometimes, Grandma would take me up to the attic—a scary and magical place. It was filled with old trunks, forgotten treasures, and the kind of mystery that only an attic can hold. I always wanted to dig through the piles of "old stuff," but we never seemed to have the time.

One Christmas, she took me into town to see the parade. The lights, music, and excitement were all so magical. Afterward, we went shopping, and she bought me my first Barbie doll. Those weekends with Grandma were the best part of my childhood.

Memory Prompts

- Did you or a friend ever play with paper dolls growing up?

- Describe a time you have been around farm animals, such as chickens or cows.

- Was there a fruit you didn't like when you had it for the first time as a child?

Chapter 15
The Zamboni

I still remember the night my dad and I went to the local ice arena to watch a hockey game. It was one of those small-town arenas that only held about 600 people, but it was packed to the rafters that night. The energy in the place was electric, with the roar of the crowd and the sharp clack of hockey sticks echoing through the cold air. As a little kid, though, I'll admit that the game itself couldn't hold my attention for long. I was more interested in the popcorn, the atmosphere, and, most of all, the Zamboni.

For some reason, I was completely fascinated by that big, lumbering machine. Of all the vehicles a kid could fall in love with—fire trucks, race cars, airplanes—the Zamboni was my absolute favorite. I loved how it would glide over the ice, this giant boxy thing that magically smoothed out the rough, snowy surface, leaving behind a glassy, pristine sheet. The Zamboni wasn't just part of the game—it made the game possible.

After the first period, my dad nudged me that night and pointed at a sign announcing a special drawing. The winner would get to ride the Zamboni during the ice cut after the second period. I didn't think much of it, but my dad, knowing how much I loved that machine, entered my name. I didn't think we'd win, but a kid can dream.

As the second period wound down, I was only half paying attention when the announcer came on the loudspeaker. My dad's hand suddenly gripped my shoulder. "Listen up!" he said, his voice full of excitement. They were reading off the winning ticket number, and as the announcer called out the digits, I realized they matched the one in my dad's hand. We had won. I could hardly believe it.

From that moment on, I couldn't sit still. The last few minutes of the period felt like an eternity. I kept glancing at the Zamboni doors, nervous and excited. When the clock finally ticked to 30 seconds left, my dad and I made our way to the rink's edge. But when we got there, no one was waiting for us. My heart sank—I was terrified that maybe something had gone wrong, that I wouldn't get my ride after all.

And then, just as the period ended, the Zamboni garage door started to creak open. There it was, the Zamboni, sitting in all its glory, bathed in the arena's bright lights. The driver, a friendly-looking guy in an oversized jacket, leaned out and asked, "You ready, kid?"

"Yes!" I said, trying to contain my excitement as he lifted me onto the seat. As the Zamboni rumbled to life beneath me, I felt like I was on top of the world.

He put it in reverse, and we slowly backed out of the dark garage and into the blinding light and noise of the arena. It was overwhelming—in the best way possible. The announcer called out my name, and I could hear the crowd cheering and feel all those eyes watching me. The hum of the

Zamboni's conditioners and the sheer thrill of being on the ice hit me at once, flooding my senses.

We did the ice cut, and all too soon, the ride was over. The driver helped me down, and I floated back to my seat. I watched the rest of the game with a new sense of wonder. I felt like the luckiest kid in the world that night, winning that Zamboni ride.

Memory Prompts

- Have you ever won a special prize or contest as a child? How did it make you feel?

- Did you have a favorite place to visit or activity in your hometown as a child? What was it?

- Was there ever a vehicle or machine that fascinated you as a child? What drew you to it?

Chapter 16

Perfume and Pioneers

When my sisters and I were little, the world was our playground, and our imaginations knew no bounds. It was the summer of 1967, and at ages five, six, and eight, we spent our days lost in make-believe adventures. Our favorite game was "Pioneers," where we'd transform our backyard into the untamed frontier, complete with covered wagons, wild animals, and, of course, all the necessities we thought pioneers would need.

One warm afternoon, as we roamed our backyard, we decided we needed to make perfume—because, naturally, that's what pioneers did. It made perfect sense to us at the time. We were determined to create something beautiful and fragrant that our imaginary pioneer mothers would be proud of.

Our first task was to find the perfect container for our concoction. We rummaged through the garage and finally settled on a large white bucket. It was a bit weathered, with a few dents and scratches, but to us, it was the ideal vessel for our pioneer perfume.

Next, we needed ingredients. We ran around the yard, picking as many flowers as possible. Dandelions, daisies, wild clover—anything that bloomed was fair game. We piled our floral treasures into the bucket, delighted with our colorful collection.

Once we had gathered enough flowers, we filled the bucket with water from the garden hose. The cold, clear water splashed over the petals, creating a mix of vibrant colors swirling around. The sight of it made us giggle with excitement.

"We need a stick to stir it!" my older sister declared, taking charge as usual. She always knew what to do.

We scoured the yard until we found the perfect stick—a long, sturdy branch that had fallen from the old oak tree. One by one, we took turns stirring our floral concoction, watching as the petals danced in the water, the colors blending in a fragrant brew. We were serious about our work, each of us giving the mixture a good stir for what felt like hours but was probably only about thirty minutes.

"This is going to be the best perfume ever," I said, my tiny hands gripping the stick as I gave the bucket one final stir.

When we were satisfied that our perfume was ready, we dipped our fingers into the bucket and brought them to our noses. The scent wasn't exactly what we had imagined—more earthy than floral, with a hint of something green—but to us, it was perfect. We had created something from nothing, just like the pioneers we admired so much.

We spent the rest of the afternoon proudly "selling" our perfume to each other, exchanging imaginary coins for imaginary bottles while basking in the joy of our simple creation.

Those afternoons spent playing pioneers, making perfume, and using our imaginations to create whole worlds were the foundation of a lifetime of memories. And though the perfume we made that day was fleeting, the memory of our adventure has lasted a lifetime.

Memory Prompts

- Do you have a memory of making something with your siblings or friends that still brings a smile to your face?

- Was there a particular time when your imagination led to a memorable adventure or project? What was it?

- What were your favorite plants or flowers that grew in your neighborhood?

Chapter 17

Flashlight Tag

When I was growing up, my friends in the neighborhood and I would play flashlight tag. The cul-de-sac was the perfect playground for a group of kids with boundless energy. There were no fences to separate our yards, no busy streets to keep us in check—just a wide-open stretch of grass, a few scattered trees, and the woods that loomed behind our houses.

The best nights for flashlight tag were those warm evenings when the sun lingered just long enough to let us eat dinner outside before it slipped below the horizon. As soon as darkness fell, the game would begin. Armed with flashlights and a sense of adventure, we'd gather in the center of the cul-de-sac, our breathless excitement barely contained.

"Okay, who's 'It'?" one of the kids asked.

"I'll be 'It,'" I volunteered, feeling a thrill of anticipation. Being 'It' meant you had the power to seek out the hidden, to catch the flash of a sneaker in the grass, or to chase the rustle of leaves in the woods.

With the roles decided, everyone scattered, their flashlights clicking off as they disappeared into the shadows. The only sound was the chorus of crickets and the occasional whisper of a breeze through the trees. I stood alone for a moment, listening, trying to pick up any hint of movement.

Then, with a flick of the switch, my flashlight beam cut through the darkness. I began to move slowly at first, sweeping the light across the yards and the edge of the woods. The thrill of the hunt made my heart pound in my chest. Somewhere out there, my friends were crouched in the shadows, waiting, hoping they wouldn't be found.

The beam of my flashlight caught something—a quick flash of white, the hem of a T-shirt, darting behind a tree. I grinned and ran toward it, knowing I was close.

"Gotcha!" I shouted as my light found one of my neighbors, Billy, his eyes wide in surprise.

"Ah, you got me," he laughed, standing up and brushing the grass off his jeans. "But you'll never catch the others—they're way better at hiding."

We teamed up, our flashlights cutting through the night as we searched for the rest of the gang. One by one, we found them—under the porch, behind the old oak tree, lying flat in the tall grass. Each discovery was met with a mix of laughter and groans.

Eventually, everyone was caught, and we returned to the center of the cul-de-sac, out of breath but exhilarated. We sat in a circle, flashlights shining upward, casting eerie shadows on our faces as we told stories and made plans for the next round.

We played until our parents called us home, their voices mingling with the night sounds. All these years later, when I think back to those nights, I can still feel the pure, uncomplicated joy of being a kid playing flashlight tag with my friends, and I miss it dearly.

Memory Prompts

- What memories do you have of playing outside after dark? How did it feel to play in the night?

- Was there a particular spot in your neighborhood or yard where you loved to play or hide? What made it special?

- Have you ever had a favorite childhood game that you miss playing as an adult? What do you miss most about it?

Chapter 18
My First Job

As I stood outside the local diner, nervously adjusting my tie, I couldn't shake the butterflies in my stomach. It was the summer of 1968, and this was my first real job at sixteen. The sign above the door, "Bev's Diner," flickered slightly, but it might as well have been the entrance to a whole new world.

Taking a deep breath, I pushed open the door and stepped inside. The scent of frying bacon and fresh coffee filled the air, mingling with the low hum of conversation and the clatter of dishes. Behind the counter, I spotted Bev herself, a short woman with a kind smile, who waved me over.

"You must be Kevin," she said, wiping her hands on her apron. "Glad you're here, hon. We'll start you off with bussing tables. You think you can handle that?"

I nodded, my heart racing. "Yes, ma'am. I'll do my best."

The first few hours were a blur as I moved through the diner like a whirlwind, clearing plates, refilling coffee cups, and trying not to bump into the waiters and waitresses who rushed past with trays piled high with food. It was more complicated than it looked, but I was determined to prove myself.

Around lunchtime, the diner filled up, and the pace quickened. I struggled to keep up when a plate of spaghetti slipped from my hands, crashing to the floor in a mess of sauce and noodles. The entire diner seemed to go silent, and I felt my face flush with embarrassment.

Before I could even bend down to clean it up, Bev was beside me, a warm hand on my shoulder. "It's okay, Kevin," she said gently. "Accidents happen. Just clean it up and keep going. You're doing fine."

Her words were exactly what I needed to hear. I quickly grabbed a rag and cleaned up the mess, grateful that Bev didn't make a big deal out of it. As the day wore on, I found my rhythm improving with each table I cleared.

By the time my shift ended, I was exhausted but proud. I had survived my first day, and despite the mishap with the spaghetti, I felt like I had done a pretty good job.

As I was about to leave, Bev called me over. "Kevin, wait a minute," she said, handing me a soda. "You did well today. Working in a place like this is not easy, especially when it's busy. But you kept going, even after the accident. That's what matters."

"Thank you, Bev," I said, taking the soda with a grateful smile. "I'll do better tomorrow."

I walked home that evening, relieved that I had survived my first day. Tomorrow, I'd be back at the diner, ready to work harder, learn more, and keep going.

Memory Prompts

- Describe the first job you ever had. What did you like or dislike about it?

- Have you ever worked at a restaurant or retail store?

- Share one lesson in life you learned at work.

Chapter 19

The Gift of Gymnastics

Gymnastics had always been my world. I was hooked when my mom took me to that first toddler class when I was three. There was something magical about how my body could move, the thrill of flipping through the air, and the sheer joy of sticking a landing. But life, as it often does, threw a curveball when I was seven. My mom, a single parent working tirelessly to make ends meet, could no longer keep up with my gymnastics classes' increasing costs and time demands. The day she told me we had to stop going to the gym was one of the hardest of my young life.

At the time, I couldn't understand why something I loved so much had to be taken away. I felt like a part of me was missing, and although the ache eventually dulled, it never really went away. I stopped thinking about gymnastics as much, but every time I saw a gymnast on TV or heard someone talking about the sport, that old longing would resurface.

But then, on my eleventh birthday, something unexpected happened. Instead of taking the bus home like I usually did, my mom picked me up early. She greeted me with a smile, but I could tell she had something up her sleeve. "Close your eyes," she said, her voice filled with excitement. "I have a surprise for you."

I had no idea what to expect, but I did as she asked, shutting my eyes tightly as we drove. The car ride lasted forever, my curiosity growing with each passing minute. Finally, the car stopped, and my mom told me I could open my eyes.

When I did, I couldn't believe what I saw. We were parked in front of the gym, the same one I had left behind four years earlier. My heart skipped a beat as I turned to my mom, her eyes shining with the joy of seeing my reaction.

"We're back," she said, her voice soft and full of love. "I'm signing you up for gymnastics classes again. For real this time."

Tears welled up in my eyes as the weight of her words sank in. I was going back to the gym—the place where I had felt happiest, the place where I could be myself. It was more than just a birthday present. It was the gift of a dream revived, a second chance to do what I loved.

That day marked the beginning of a new chapter in my life. Over the next seven years, gymnastics became my refuge, passion, and purpose. I worked harder than ever, pushing myself to new limits and achieving things I had once only dreamed of. I met Olympians, trained with one of the most renowned coaches in the sport, and traveled across the country, competing in events that took my breath away.

And in one unforgettable moment, I stood on the podium as a national champion in uneven bars—a title that symbolized victory and the journey that had brought me there.

Gymnastics saved me in more ways than I can describe. It gave me the strength to push through the darkest times and the determination to keep going, no matter what. And it all started with that one birthday gift from my mother, who never stopped believing and supporting me. It was, without a doubt, the gift of a lifetime.

Memory Prompts

- Was there ever a hobby or activity you loved as a child that you had to give up? How did it feel, and did you ever return to it?

- Have you ever experienced a moment when a second chance or opportunity changed the course of your life? What was it?

- What was a passion or dream you had as a child that shaped who you are today?

Chapter 20

Grandma's Kitchen and the Throne

My Grandma's kitchen was filled with warmth and love, and the irresistible scent of something delicious was always simmering on the stove. Grandma had a way of making every visit to her house feel like a special occasion, and she always had a little something up her sleeve to make me feel like royalty.

One of my favorite traditions was when Grandma would teach me how to make her famous brown sugar fudge. It was a family recipe passed down through generations, and she was determined to share it with me. The kitchen would come alive with the clinking of spoons and the soft bubbling of the sugar mixture, and I felt like I was part of something magical.

"Come on, love," she'd say, tying an apron around my waist. "It's time to make some fudge. You remember the steps?"

I'd nod eagerly, though I could never quite remember everything. But that didn't matter—Grandma was always there to guide me as we measured the ingredients.

First came the brown sugar, then the butter, melting together in a saucepan over the stove. The aroma of the caramelizing sugar filled the kitchen, making my mouth water. Grandma's eyes would twinkle as she handed me the spoon.

I'd take the spoon and stir, carefully following her guidance. The mixture would turn thick and creamy, bubbling gently as it came together.

Once the fudge was ready, we'd pour it into a buttered pan, smoothing it until it was perfectly even. Then came the hardest part—waiting for it to cool. I'd sit there, watching the fudge intently, as if my eyes could make it set faster.

While we waited, Grandma would pull out her old recliner, which she'd lovingly turned into my "throne." It was a worn, comfy chair with a blanket draped over the back, and whenever I visited, it became my special seat. She'd let me climb into it, arranging the blanket around me like a royal robe.

"There you go, Your Highness," she'd say with a grin. "The throne is all yours."

I'd giggle and settle into the chair, feeling like the queen of the world. And while I held court on my throne, Grandma would slip away to her room and return with a small jar filled with coins. It was her secret stash, saved up just for me.

"Here you go, darling," she'd say, handing me the jar. "A little spending money for when we go to the store later."

NOSTALGIC SHORT STORIES FOR SENIORS

The jar would jingle with nickels, dimes, and the occasional quarter, and I'd hold it close, already imagining what I might buy. To a child, it felt like a treasure chest.

Finally, the fudge would be ready, and Grandma would cut me a piece and pack the rest for me to take home to share. We'd sit together in the kitchen, savoring the rich, sweet treat.

Those afternoons in Grandma's kitchen, with the smell of brown sugar in the air, were some of the happiest times of my life. When I'm stressed, I like to think about my Grandma's kitchen and my "throne."

Memory Prompts

- Do you have a favorite family recipe that was passed down to you? What makes it special?

- Did you have a favorite chair or special spot in your house growing up?

- Was there a dessert you associate with your childhood?

Chapter 21

Christmas Morning Traditions

Christmas morning was always the most magical time of the year in our house. The anticipation of the day, the twinkling lights on the tree, and the aroma of cinnamon rolls baking in the oven made it feel like we were living in a holiday movie. But what made our Christmas mornings truly special were the traditions we followed without fail—watching *A Christmas Story* and tuning in to the Macy's Christmas Parade.

I can still remember the thrill of waking up early, the soft glow of the tree lights casting a warm, festive hue over the living room. My siblings and I would creep down the stairs, trying to keep quiet, but the creaky steps always gave us away.

"Go on and wake up mom and dad," my older sister would whisper, nudging me with a grin. "It's Christmas morning!"

Once everyone was gathered, still in our pajamas, we'd start the morning with a breakfast feast. Mom always had a spread of cinnamon rolls, bacon, and fresh orange juice ready for us.

Dad would load the VHS tape into the player, and as soon as the opening credits began to roll, we'd all get comfortable on the couch, blankets piled high. There was something comforting about the familiarity of it all. We knew every line and every scene, but it never got old. We'd laugh in anticipation before the jokes even landed—Ralphie's wild imagination, the leg lamp fiasco, and of course, the infamous "triple dog dare."

The movie was more than just entertainment—it was the thread that connected our Christmases year after year, a reminder of the joy and laughter that defined our family.

As soon as the credits rolled and Ralphie drifted off to sleep with his Red Ryder BB gun, Dad would switch over to the Macy's Christmas Parade. The grand spectacle of it all never failed to captivate us. We'd watch in awe as the giant balloons floated down the streets of New York City, their vibrant colors and larger-than-life characters filling our living room with wonder.

"Look, there's Snoopy!" my little sister would squeal, pointing excitedly at the screen.

"And here come the Rockettes!" Mom would add, her voice tinged with nostalgia. "They're always my favorite."

We'd spend the next few hours watching the parade, commenting on the elaborate floats, the marching bands, and the celebrities waving to the crowds. It was like being part of something bigger than ourselves, a connection to the world outside our cozy home, where people everywhere celebrated the same joyful day.

By the time Santa Claus made his grand entrance, signaling the end of the parade, we were all filled with the holiday spirit, ready to dive into the gift-giving and festivities that awaited us.

As the years passed, our Christmas mornings stayed the same. The world outside changed, and we all grew up, but those traditions remained a constant source of comfort and happiness. Even now, we try to watch *A Christmas Story* and the Macy's Christmas Parade on Christmas morning, passing the tradition down to the next generation.

For us, those simple rituals are more than just a way to celebrate the holiday—they're a reminder of the magic of our family's Christmas mornings.

Memory Prompts

- Is there a particular movie or show that you watch every year during the holidays? How does it make you feel?

- What are some of the small rituals or traditions that make your holiday celebrations unique?

- Can you recall a holiday memory that brings you joy whenever you think about it? What happened?

Chapter 22

Waffles and Sausages

Some of my fondest childhood memories are of weekends spent with my Grandpa. His house was a cozy haven with the soft hum of the radio playing old tunes in the background. But the best part of those weekends, which still warms my heart today, was waking up to the smell of his cooking.

I'd wake up in the small, sunlit guest room, and the first thing I'd notice was the mouthwatering aroma drifting from the kitchen. It was a smell I'd recognize anywhere: the rich, buttery scent of freshly made waffles mingling with the savory aroma of sausages sizzling on the stove.

I'd hop out of bed and rush down the stairs, my excitement growing with every step. Grandpa would already be in the kitchen, standing at the stove with a smile that lit up his face. He always wore the same thing—his favorite plaid shirt, sleeves rolled up, and an apron that had seen better days but was worn with love.

"Morning, sunshine," he'd greet me, his voice warm and full of affection. "Hope you're hungry."

"Always, Grandpa!" I'd reply, sliding into my usual seat at the kitchen table.

On the stove, the sausages would be cooking in his unique way—boiled first, then fried to perfection. They were small and crispy, just the right size for my little hands. No store-bought sausage has ever come close to the ones he made. They had a taste that was pure magic, a blend of spices and care that made each bite better than the last.

And then there were the waffles. Oh, those waffles. Grandpa had an old, well-used waffle iron that he treated like gold. He'd pour the batter in precisely, closing the lid and waiting just the right amount of time before lifting it to reveal golden, fluffy waffles with perfectly crisp edges. He always made them just the way I liked—soft in the middle, with a hint of vanilla.

He'd set the plate in front of me, the waffles steaming, a small mountain of sausages piled on the side. And without fail, he'd say, "Dig in, kiddo. You're growing faster than I can keep up with."

I'd drown the waffles in syrup, then take that first bite, savoring the combination of sweet and savory, the crispy and soft textures mingling together. Every bite was a little piece of heaven, made all the more special because Grandpa had made it just for me.

We'd sit together, me devouring the food like I hadn't eaten in days and him watching with a satisfied smile, sipping his coffee. Those breakfasts were more than just meals—they were moments of pure love and connection, a time when the world outside didn't matter, and all that existed was the kitchen's warmth and the bond between us.

Now, whenever I smell waffles cooking or sausages frying, I'm taken back to those mornings in my Grandpa's kitchen, to the sound of him humming a tune while he cooked. No waffle or sausage ever tastes as good as the ones Grandpa made for me. Grandpa was a great man, and in those simple, delicious breakfasts, he gave me something I'll cherish forever—a taste of love that's as warm and comforting as the memory itself.

Memory Prompts

- What was your favorite breakfast as a child, and who usually made it for you?

- What sauce or syrup do you like to eat with waffles and sausages?

- Do you remember a time when someone made you feel especially loved through a simple act, like cooking a meal?

Chapter 23

Sunday Dinner

As a third-generation Italian, Sundays weren't just another day of the week—they were a day of tradition, family, and, most importantly, food. From the moment you walked through the door, the aroma of simmering sauce and freshly baked bread wrapped around you like a warm embrace.

The day always started with antipasto. And not just any antipasto—it was a spread that could rival the best Italian deli. There was capicola, prosciutto, and hot sopressata (it had to be the hot kind—nothing else would do). We'd pile our plates high with fresh mozzarella, the kind that practically melted in your mouth, and thick slices of semolina bread from the good bakery down the street. There were olives, roasted peppers, and the pièce de résistance—a jar of our homemade super spicy eggplant.

The first course was always a salad, but not just any salad. Gram made it with red leaf lettuce and tossed it in a balsamic vinaigrette that was both tangy and sweet, which was the perfect balance. She'd add tomatoes, cucumbers, and whatever veggies were in season, sometimes eggplant parm or roasted zucchini if she felt fancy. There was a simplicity to it, yet it tasted like a celebration of the earth's bounty, a reminder that even the simplest things can bring immense joy.

Then came the main event—the sauce, never "gravy," as some might call it. It was rich and hearty, with meatballs, sausage, and braciole, each piece simmered to perfection. And if it was a special occasion, we were treated to veal cutlets, tender and golden brown. Rigatoni was the pasta of choice, its ridges perfect for holding onto every drop of that glorious sauce. We'd pass around pecorino Romano bowls and ricotta dollops, letting everyone customize their plates just the way they liked it.

If the weather was nice, we'd take the party outside, where skirt steak sizzled on the grill, its smoky aroma mingling with the summer breeze. Afterward, we'd dive into thick, juicy watermelon slices, the perfect ending to a perfect meal. But if the weather kept us indoors, we'd finish with Gram's homemade cannoli and an assortment of cookies. And, of course, no meal was complete without a cup of espresso with a splash of Sambuca, its anise flavor lingering.

Even now, decades later, the memories of those Sundays at Gram's house are as vivid as ever. Each bite was a connection to our roots; each dinner reminded us of the bonds that held us together. I wish we could continue the tradition; nothing comes close to being as good as those Sunday dinners.

Memory Prompts

- Did your family have a special day of the week dedicated to traditions or gatherings? What made it unique?

- How did your family's cultural background influence the meals or traditions in your home?

- Do you have any food-related traditions that you've passed down to your own children or grandchildren?

Chapter 24

Walks on the Pier

Growing up, some of my fondest memories were made at the pier near our home. It was a place of simple joys, where the sea breeze was always fresh, and the sun seemed to shine a little brighter. My parents and I would often spend our weekends there, walking the long stretch of wooden planks, watching the waves crash beneath us, and soaking in the ocean's sights and sounds.

I must have been about seven or eight when these weekend outings became a cherished tradition. Hand in hand with my parents, I'd skip along the boards, my eyes wide with excitement as we approached the fishermen who lined the railings. Their weathered faces and steady hands fascinated me. They always seemed so focused and patient as they cast their lines into the deep blue waters, waiting for a bite.

"Look, Daddy!" I'd exclaim, pointing at the wriggling fish one of the men had just pulled from the sea. "Did he catch that all by himself?"

My father would chuckle, nodding. "He sure did! It takes a lot of practice to catch fish like that."

Sometimes, the fishermen would smile at me, their eyes crinkling in the corners, and they'd hold up their catches for me to see—a shiny silver mackerel, a flounder with its flat, funny shape, or even a tiny crab that had gotten tangled in the net.

After exploring the pier, we'd make our way to the end, where a small diner named Ruby's stood like a beacon of warmth and welcome. To my young eyes, Ruby's was the height of sophistication. Its red-and-white striped awnings and vintage décor made it feel like a place out of a storybook, a special spot reserved just for us.

"Are we going to eat at Ruby's tonight?" I'd ask eagerly, already imagining the treat that awaited me.

My mother would smile and nod, knowing how much I loved our tradition. "Of course, honey. What would a trip to the pier be without dinner at Ruby's?"

We'd settle into a booth by the window, where we could still see the ocean stretching to the horizon. The menu was simple—burgers, fries, and sandwiches—but to me, it was a feast fit for royalty. My parents would order their meals, and I'd always get the same thing: a cheeseburger, fries, and a chocolate milkshake with a cherry on top.

When the milkshake arrived, I'd carefully pluck the cherry from the whipped cream and savor it slowly as if it were the most luxurious treat in the world. Those walks on the pier with my parents, the fishermen's friendly smiles, and the milkshakes at Ruby's are the small things that made life feel rich and full growing up.

Memory Prompts

- Have you ever gone fishing? If so, did you go fishing at a river, lake, or pier?

- What flavor of ice cream or milkshake do you enjoy? Do you prefer it with whipped cream and a cherry on top?

- Did you ever have a favorite restaurant or diner growing up that felt like a special treat to visit? What did you love about it?

Chapter 25

Polaroid Moments

One Christmas morning, I could hardly contain my excitement. The living room was filled with the scent of pine, and the twinkling lights from the tree cast a warm, magical glow over everything. Wrapping paper and ribbons were scattered across the floor, but one gift still sat under the tree with my name on it.

My parents exchanged a knowing smile as I reached for the shiny red box adorned with a big gold bow. My fingers trembled with anticipation as I carefully unwrapped it, revealing a Polaroid OneStep Camera.

"Is this...?" My voice trailed off in disbelief.

"It sure is," my dad said, beaming. "Now you can take all the pictures you've always wanted."

My heart swelled with joy as I lifted the sleek, white camera from the box. I had admired Polaroid cameras in magazines for so long but never imagined I would own one.

"Thank you so much!" I exclaimed, jumping up to hug my parents.

My mom laughed. "We knew you'd love it. Now, how about you take the first picture?"

I fumbled a bit as I loaded the film, my excitement nearly overwhelming me. Once ready, I held the camera up and looked through the viewfinder. My parents smiled back at me, seated by the tree, while my little brother, Manny, played on the floor with crumpled wrapping paper.

"Say cheese!" I called out, pressing the button.

The camera whirred softly, and a square photo ejected. I watched in awe as the image slowly developed, revealing my parents and Manny, their expressions filled with warmth and happiness.

"It works!" I cried, holding up the photo. "Look at this!"

My parents marveled at the picture, and I felt a surge of excitement. This camera was more than just a gadget; it was a way to capture the world around me, preserving the moments that meant the most.

From that day on, I took my camera everywhere—to school, the park, and the local diner where my friends and I gathered after classes. Each photo became a snapshot of my youth, a glimpse into the simple joys of growing up.

I captured birthdays with glowing candles and friends laughing as they sang. I snapped pictures of Manny playing in the yard with his toy trucks, his face smudged with dirt and pure delight. Family gatherings, where the sun shone bright, and the food tasted better because we were together, became treasured memories on film.

I found beauty in everyday moments, too—my mom making dough for empanadas in the kitchen, my dad mowing the grass outside. Each photograph was a piece of my life, a memory I could hold. As the years passed, my collection grew, carefully preserved in albums.

Many years later, I sat by the window with my old Polaroid camera resting on my lap, flipping through an album of my earliest pictures. Although my Polaroid was no longer working, the images it had produced were just as vivid as the day I captured them. I smiled as I came across that first picture of my parents and Manny.

Memory Prompts

- Did you ever have a Polaroid camera growing up? If so, did you like using it?

- Picture in your mind one of your favorite pictures from childhood. Describe who or what is in the picture.

- If you were to have your picture taken right now, how would you take it? Strike a pose and a smile.

Chapter 26

Swinging into Friendship

When I moved to the United States from Venezuela at the age of seven, I was overwhelmed by the newness of it all—the unfamiliar sights, sounds, and especially the language. Not knowing a word of English made the transition even harder. I felt like an outsider, lost in a world that didn't understand me and one I couldn't understand.

Our new neighborhood was filled with children my age, but I didn't know how to approach them. The language barrier felt insurmountable, so I kept to myself. Every afternoon, I would walk to the playground in our neighborhood, where I'd spend hours on the swings, my small refuge. The rhythm of swinging back and forth was comforting, a way to pass the time in this strange, new place.

As the days turned into weeks, I started to pick up bits and pieces of English. My parents had enrolled me in school, where I was slowly learning the basics. Words and phrases began to make sense, but I still didn't have the confidence to speak to the other kids. Instead, I watched them from a distance, swinging higher and higher, feeling both close and far from their world.

One sunny afternoon, a boy around my age approached me as I was daydreaming on the swings. His hair was tousled from running around, and his face was flushed with excitement. He stopped in front of me, catching his breath, and said something that made my heart race with anxiety and curiosity.

"Do you want to play tag?"

I understood the question, but the words felt foreign on my tongue. My heart pounded as I considered what to say. I knew this was a chance—a chance to make a friend, to be part of the group I'd been watching from afar.

"Yes," I managed to say, my voice shaky but determined. I could see the boy's eyes light up, and I felt a flicker of hope. "I... I'm Carlos," I added, my English clumsy and thick with my accent.

"Hi, Carlos! I'm Mike," he said with a big grin. "Come on, let's play!"

I was frozen with fear for a moment, unsure of what to do next. But Mike didn't give me time to overthink. He tagged my arm lightly and took off running, laughing as he went. Instinctively, I jumped off the swing and ran after him, the word "tag" now making perfect sense.

We ran around the playground, dodging and weaving through the jungle gym. My broken English didn't matter anymore. What mattered was the connection—simple, pure, and full of joy. Mike introduced me to the other kids, and soon, we were all playing together, the language barrier shrinking with every laugh and every game of tag.

That afternoon marked a turning point in my life. The swings, my solitary escape, now symbolized something much greater. They were the bridge to my first friendships in the United States. Through those simple moments of play, I learned that friendship didn't need perfect words or flawless sentences. It required only an open heart and the courage to say "yes."

Looking back, I realize that day on the playground was more than just a game of tag. It was the beginning of my journey toward belonging, a journey that started with a single word and a simple invitation. And for that, I will always be grateful.

Memory Prompts

- Have you ever had to start over in a new place? How did you find ways to connect with others?

- What was the first friendship you made as a child? How did it begin?

- Have you ever struggled to communicate with someone due to a language barrier? How did you manage to connect with them?

Chapter 27

Casper's Great Rescue

Casper, my mischievous white cat, had always been a bit of a daredevil. He loved to climb anything and everything, from the furniture in our house to the trees in the backyard. But one day, he took his adventurous spirit to a new level, leaving him stuck up a pine tree for an entire week.

It all started when Casper didn't come home one evening. At first, we thought he was just out exploring, as he often did. But worry began to set in when he didn't return the next day. We searched the neighborhood, calling his name, but no sign of him. It wasn't until a few days later that we finally heard a faint meow from the tall pine tree at the edge of our garden.

"There he is!" I shouted, spotting Casper high up in the tree, his white fur standing out against the green needles. Relief washed over me, but a sinking feeling quickly replaced it as I realized how high up he was.

The tree was one of the tallest in the neighborhood, with thin, whippy branches that looked like they could snap under the weight of a squirrel, let alone a person. None of the neighbors had a ladder tall enough to reach him, and as much as I wanted to climb up there and rescue him myself, it was clear that the tree wouldn't support me.

My mother decided to call in the professionals. But instead of dialing 999, the British equivalent of 911, she picked up the phone and called the local fire station directly.

"Hello, this is Mrs. Patel," she said, her voice calm but firm. "My son's cat is stuck up a tree, and we could use some help."

To our surprise and delight, the fire station agreed to come out. I didn't think they'd take it seriously, but within minutes, I heard the distant wail of sirens growing louder. It was like a scene out of a movie—red lights flashing, the fire engine roaring down our quiet street. And to my 14-year-old self, it was the most awesome thing ever.

The firefighters jumped out of the truck, looking every bit like heroes in their uniforms. "Where's the cat?" one of them asked, a grin on his face.

"Up there," I pointed, trying to contain my excitement.

They assessed the situation and, after a quick discussion, set up a tall extension ladder. One of the firefighters began to climb. Casper, who had been meowing, went completely silent as the firefighter approached. It was as if he knew help had finally arrived. The firefighter carefully reached out and, with a gentle coaxing, managed to get a hold of him. A few moments later, he was safely on the ground, in my arms, purring loudly as if nothing had happened.

"Thank you so much!" I said, overjoyed with relief.

"No problem, lad," the firefighter replied with a wink. "We're just glad to be of service."

That evening, as Casper curled up on my lap, safe and sound, I wondered what it would take to become a firefighter. That day, they seemed like superheroes to me, and I wanted to be like them.

Memory Prompts

- Have you ever had a pet that got into trouble or was in an adventurous situation? How did you handle it?

- Was there a time when you or someone you know had to call in professionals for help with an unusual situation? What happened?

- Can you recall a moment when someone's act of kindness or bravery greatly impacted you? What did they do?

Chapter 28

The Mistletoe Mission

In the weeks leading up to Christmas when I was six years old, my grandmother, always full of ideas that blended mischief with a dash of adventure, hatched a plan. It was the kind of plan that only she could think of and one that I was both excited and terrified to be a part of.

She pointed to the large elm tree in her yard, its branches stretching like long arms reaching the sky. "See that mistletoe up there?" she asked, her eyes sparkling. I nodded, following her gaze to the clumps of green sprigs nestled high in the tree.

"We're going to gather some mistletoe and sell it," she said, her tone making it clear that this was a project we would tackle together. She handed me an old broomstick with a hook attached to the end, then gave me a boost up into the tree.

I clambered up the tree, feeling the rough bark under my hands, the branches swaying slightly under my weight. I stretched out my arm, hooking sprig after sprig with the broomstick and tugging until they came loose, falling into the pile of greenery we had already gathered.

Inside the house, she had a red velvet ribbon waiting. We spent the afternoon tying bows around the bunches of mistletoe, creating little bouquets that looked as festive as any decoration I had seen. When we were done, she helped me load them into my Red Ryder wagon, carefully arranging them by size and the number of berries—5¢, 10¢, and 25¢ for the biggest ones.

With a mixture of excitement and nervousness, I started knocking on doors on our street. Each time, I'd hold up a bunch of mistletoe, proudly explaining that it was for sale. To my surprise, the neighbors were eager to buy, reaching into their pockets and handing me nickels, dimes, and quarters. After covering just a block and a half, I was sold out, my wagon empty, and my pockets full. I had made $3 and change—a fortune in the eyes of a six-year-old.

With it, I went to the Five & Dime and carefully picked out presents for everyone in the family. For the first time, I was able to give gifts bought with my own money, a feeling that filled me with a deep sense of joy and accomplishment.

And to this day, whenever I see mistletoe hanging in someone's home, I'm reminded of that adventure with my grandmother. The real gift that Christmas wasn't the money or the presents—it was the lesson my grandmother taught me about courage, hard work, and the satisfaction of earning something for yourself.

Memory Prompts

- Was there ever a time when you earned your own money as a child? How did it feel, and what did you do with it?

- Have you ever kissed someone under a mistletoe?

- Have you ever created or sold something you made yourself? What was the experience like?

Chapter 29

Summer Nights at the Drive-In

One of my favorite memories was the first time I went to the Starlight Drive-In. The drive-in was the heart of our town, where everyone gathered to lose themselves in a movie under the stars. My best friends Trevor and Peyton and I had been looking forward to tonight for weeks. We'd scraped together three dollars for tickets, eager to see *West Side Story*.

As the sun set, Trevor's old Chevy pulled into my driveway. I grabbed a bag of homemade popcorn and some sodas before hopping into the car.

"You ready?" Trevor called from the driver's seat.

"Born ready," I grinned, sliding in next to Peyton. "Got the popcorn and everything."

The ride to the drive-in was filled with our usual banter—talk about school, girls, and the latest songs on the radio. But as we neared the Starlight, our attention shifted to the main event.

"Think it'll be crowded?" I asked, a bit of excitement tingling in my voice.

"Probably," Trevor said with a shrug. "But that's half the fun."

We arrived at the drive-in, joining a line of cars waiting to enter. The smell of popcorn and the faint sound of music filled the air, heightening our anticipation. When we finally reached the ticket booth, Trevor handed over the three crumpled dollars, and the attendant tore off three tickets with a smile.

"Enjoy the show, boys," she said.

"Oh, we will," Trevor replied with a grin.

We found a spot near the middle, with a perfect view of the giant screen. Trevor maneuvered the Chevy into place, and we quickly set up our makeshift theater in the back of the car, piling blankets on the trunk and spreading out the popcorn and sodas. As the sky darkened, the first flickers of the movie lit up the screen.

"Here we go," Peyton said, settling in. "This is what summer's all about."

I nodded in agreement, my eyes fixed on the screen. The opening notes of *West Side Story* filled the air. There was something magical about watching a movie outdoors, under the stars.

As the movie played on, we were completely absorbed. We laughed at the jokes, gasped at the tense moments, and whispered comments to each other during the quieter scenes.

"I can't believe how good this is," I whispered, passing the popcorn to Trevor.

"Told you it'd be worth it," Trevor said, grabbing a handful.

When the movie ended, the screen faded to black, and the lot came alive with the sound of engines starting up and people chatting about the film.

"That was amazing," Trevor said as he started the car, and we nodded in agreement.

As we pulled up to my house, I paused before hopping out. "Tonight was great, guys. Let's do it again soon!"

"You bet," Peyton added. "Next time, let's make it a double feature."

I grinned as I closed the car door and waved goodbye. This night was just the first of many trips to the drive-in during my high school years. There is nothing quite like the magic of movies under the stars.

Memory Prompts

- Have you ever been to a drive-in movie theater? Did you go with friends or family?

- Name 2-3 snacks you like to eat during a movie.

- Do you like musicals or movies based on musicals, such as *West Side Story?* If so, which is your favorite?

Chapter 30

School Night Birthday

I can still remember my 9th birthday like it was yesterday. My birthday fell on a school night. While that might have seemed like it would put a damper on the day, my parents had other plans.

When I got home from school that afternoon, there was an air of excitement. My parents were waiting for me in the kitchen, their smiles warm and welcoming. "Happy Birthday, Ethan!" my dad said, ruffling my hair. My mom gave me a quick hug before saying, "We've got a surprise for you tonight."

I could hardly contain my excitement as we piled into the car. I had no idea what they had planned, but I knew it would be special—my parents always had a way of making even the simplest days feel like magic.

Our first stop was dinner at my favorite little diner. I remember the scent of burgers sizzling on the grill as we walked in, the cozy booths lining the walls, and the cheerful clatter of dishes being washed in the back. When the waitress came to take our order, I didn't even have to look at the menu. "I'll have the burger, please," I said, though the spaghetti equally tempted me. As we finished, the waitress brought out a small Carvel cake with my name in bright blue icing. I was over the moon.

After dinner, I thought we might be heading home, but instead, my dad turned the car toward the local batting cages. My eyes lit up when I realized where we were going. "Can I really?" I asked, almost not believing it.

"Of course," my mom said, smiling at me from the front seat. "It's your birthday!"

We pulled into the parking lot, and I could hardly wait to get out of the car. The batting cages were quiet that night, the machines clicking softly as they spit out baseballs. My dad handed me a bat, and I stepped into the cage, the cool evening air brushing against my face.

I remember the sound of the bat connecting with the ball, the satisfaction of watching it sail into the net, and how my parents cheered me on with every hit.

Afterward, we headed home, and as we pulled into the driveway, my mom handed me a small wrapped gift. Inside was a Mattel handheld football game, the very one I'd been eyeing in the store for weeks. My eyes widened with delight. I couldn't wait to play it, but it was getting late, and my mom reminded me that school was just a few hours away.

That night, as I drifted off to sleep, I knew I'd remember this birthday for the rest of my life. And I do—it was a nostalgic, perfect birthday on a school night.

Memory Prompts

- Do you have a favorite birthday memory from your childhood that still stands out to you? What made it special?

- Did you have a set bedtime for school nights growing up? What time did you get up for school?

- What kind of cake or dessert would you get for your birthdays growing up?

Chapter 31

The Great Coaster Battle

Growing up with two brothers was always an adventure. Our house was a battleground for the endless games we invented, each one more ridiculous than the last. But nothing quite compared to the chaos of our infamous coaster wars. It was a game that only we could have dreamed up—throwing hard cork coasters at each other like frisbees while hiding behind couches and laughing until our sides hurt.

We had about six of those coasters. They were meant to protect the coffee table from our endless parade of drinks, but to us, they were the perfect ammunition for a war that spanned the entire living room.

The rules were simple: each of us would take cover behind a couch, and the goal was to hit one of the other two with a flying coaster. There were no teams, no alliances—just pure, unfiltered chaos. We'd peek out from our hiding spots, waiting for the perfect moment to strike, then launch a coaster across the room, hoping to catch a brother off guard.

It was all fun and games until I accidentally became a sharpshooter.

I remember it like it was yesterday. My youngest brother, just three years younger than me, was crouched behind the couch, peeking over the edge with that mischievous glint in his eye. I saw my chance. I aimed, took a deep breath, and let the coaster fly.

But just as the coaster left my hand, he popped his head up—right into the path of my perfectly aimed shot. The coaster hit him square between the eyes, and time seemed to stand still. His eyes widened in shock, and then the blood started to pour from his nose.

I didn't wait to see his reaction. I turned and bolted for my bedroom, slamming the door shut behind me and throwing my weight against it. I could hear him pounding down the hallway, and within seconds, he was pushing against the door, trying to get in. But I had braced myself against the bed, and he couldn't budge it.

For a moment, everything went quiet. I held my breath, wondering if maybe—just maybe—he had given up. But just as I was about to relax, the quiet was shattered by a loud crash. The end of the ladder from his bunk bed came flying through the door, missing my head by inches.

I stared at the hole in the door, my heart pounding. We both knew we were in big trouble now. Our Mom would be home soon, and there was no way we could hide this.

But we tried anyway. In a moment of brotherly collaboration, we grabbed some posters from my room and taped them over the hole. We stepped back, admiring our work, convinced we had pulled off the perfect cover-up.

Of course, we hadn't fooled anyone. The second Mom walked through the door, she spotted our shoddy attempt at concealment. Her face said it all—disbelief, followed by that stern, no-nonsense look that meant we were in for it.

And in for it, we were. We were grounded for weeks, and the coaster war was suspended. But even as we sat in our rooms, punished for our mischief, we couldn't help but laugh about the whole thing.

Years later, that hole in the door became one of our favorite stories. And even though we had our fair share of battles, that day reminded me of something important: no matter how many fights we got into, we were always in it together.

Memory Prompts

- Did you and your siblings or friends have any imaginative or mischievous games you loved to play? What made them so fun?

- Was there a time when you got into trouble as a child that you can laugh about now? What happened?

- Do you have a favorite memory of a time when you and your siblings worked together, even if it was to cover up something you'd done?

Chapter 32

Saturday Mornings at Denny's

Saturday mornings were always my favorite part of the week as a kid. It wasn't just because it was the weekend or because I didn't have to go to school—it was because of the special tradition my dad, my little sister, and I had. Before my mom woke up every Saturday, we'd walk to Denny's for breakfast. It was our little ritual, just the three of us, and I looked forward to it all week.

My dad would usually bring his harmonica tucked away in his jacket pocket. He was a Civil War reenactor and loved to play old songs from that era. As we strolled down the quiet streets, he'd start playing those familiar tunes my sister and I had heard a hundred times before but never tired of. "The Battle Hymn of the Republic," "Dixie," and other melodies that carried the weight of history yet felt light and joyful in the morning air.

Of course, we knew all the words and sang along without hesitation. "Glory, glory, hallelujah!" we'd belt out, our voices rising above the hum of the harmonica. My sister would giggle whenever we messed up the lyrics, and we'd make silly faces at each other, trying to outdo one another in our attempts to be funny.

By the time we reached Denny's, we were usually in high spirits, our laughter echoing as we pushed open the door. The warm scent of pancakes and coffee would greet us, and we'd slide into our favorite booth by the window. The waitress knew us by then, always bringing extra napkins and a small cup of creamer for my sister to play with.

Breakfast was a simple affair—pancakes for me, scrambled eggs for my sister, and a stack of bacon for my dad. But it wasn't really about the food. It was about the time we spent together, how my dad would tell stories or ask us about our week, and how we'd all try to make each other laugh. We'd talk about anything and everything, from the silliest jokes to the latest Wile E. Coyote mishap on Looney Tunes.

After breakfast, we'd walk back home, still singing and talking, sometimes with my dad playing another tune on his harmonica. The neighborhood would slowly come to life around us, but we were in our own little world, connected by those simple moments of joy.

When we got home, the tradition wasn't over yet. We'd gather in front of the TV, still in our pajamas, and watch Looney Tunes. My dad loved those cartoons just as much as we did, maybe even more. I can still hear his laughter, deep and hearty, as Wile E. Coyote's latest scheme inevitably backfired.

Those Saturday mornings were idyllic to me. Whenever I get stressed in the hustle and bustle of life nowadays, I think about those mornings. It was just us together, enjoying each other's company, with nothing to worry about and nowhere else we needed to be.

Memory Prompts

- Did you have a tradition growing up that revolved around cartoons?

- Did you watch the Looney Tunes growing up? Which character was your favorite?

- Did you have a special weekend tradition with your family as a child? What made it meaningful to you?

Chapter 33

Ice Cream Truck Jingle

Summer, to me, is symbolized by the sound of the ice cream truck from my childhood with a cheerful jingle that promises sweet relief from the summer heat. And it wasn't just any ice cream truck—it was a green one, a bit worn around the edges but magical to us kids. It rolled down our street every day without fail, and like clockwork, my brother, sister, and I would rush outside, clutching our coins, eager to see what treat we could get that day.

One day, though, we missed it. I can't remember exactly why—maybe it was a doctor's appointment or just one of those days filled with errands—but as the afternoon sun began to set, I realized with a pang of disappointment that we hadn't heard the familiar tune. But then, something incredible happened.

We heard it around 8 o'clock that night—the unmistakable jingle of the ice cream truck. But this time, it was different. The music seemed to float in the air, almost magical in the way it called to us. My brother and sister and I exchanged wide-eyed looks. Could it be?

We raced to the window, and there it was: the green ice cream truck, bathed in a soft glow from lights.

"Is that...?" my sister began, her voice full of wonder.

"It is!" I shouted, already bolting for the door.

We burst outside, our excitement bubbling over as we ran toward the truck. The driver, a kind man with a warm smile, was waiting for us. He leaned out of the window and said, "I noticed you kids didn't come out today. That's not like you, so I thought I'd swing by again just to make sure everything was okay."

I couldn't believe it. He had come back just for us. It was as if he knew how much that daily visit meant to us and how those moments of choosing between a Bomb Pop or a Choco Taco were the highlights of our summer days.

"Thank you!" my brother said, his eyes wide with gratitude as he handed over his coins.

We each picked out our favorite treat, the joy of the moment making the ice cream taste even better. We sat on the porch steps, our hearts full and our hands sticky with melted ice cream. I remember looking up at the stars, feeling like the luckiest kid in the world. It wasn't just about the ice cream. It was about being seen, about someone noticing our absence and caring enough to make the extra trip. It was a small act, but it meant the world to us.

Memory Prompts

- Did you have a neighborhood ice cream truck? Do you remember the jingle it would play?

- What was your favorite ice cream treat growing up? Is it still your favorite ice cream today?

- Have you ever experienced a moment when someone went out of their way to do something kind for you? How did it affect you?

Chapter 34

Best Dentist Trip Ever

It was a regular day in fourth grade, or at least that's what I thought. We were in the middle of math class when the intercom crackled to life, and I heard my name being called. "Please send Nick Nguyen to the office—his mom is here to pick him up."

My heart sank. There was only one reason my mom would pick me up in the middle of the day: a dentist appointment. I hated going to the dentist. The thought of that sterile office, the smell of antiseptic, and the sound of those awful drills made my stomach churn. I dragged my feet to the office, already dreading the trip.

When I got there, my mom was waiting with a smile that seemed way too cheerful for a dentist visit. "We have to go to the dentist," she said, and I groaned internally, trying to muster the enthusiasm to smile back.

We got into the car, and I settled into the passenger seat, bracing myself for the inevitable. As we drove, I let my mind wander, staring out the window and trying to think of anything but the dentist. The familiar streets rolled by, and I zoned out, counting the minutes until we'd pull up to that dreaded office.

But then something strange happened. Instead of turning left towards the dentist, we kept going straight. I blinked, trying to figure out if I'd lost track of where we were. Then, before I knew it, we were pulling up to the Ballpark in Arlington, the home of the Texas Rangers.

I turned to my mom, my confusion clear on my face. "Mom, what are we doing here?"

She smiled, a mischievous twinkle in her eye. "I was joking about the dentist," she said, her grin widening. "I got us tickets to the Home Run Derby for the All-Star game this year!"

I stared at her, my mouth hanging open in shock. "Are you serious?"

"Yep!" she replied, pulling out two tickets from her purse and handing them to me. "Come on, let's go have some fun."

We walked into the stadium, the roar of the crowd and the smell of hot dogs and popcorn filling the air. It felt like I had just stepped into another world. My mom handed me my glove and said, "Go run around and see if you can catch a ball. Have fun!"

And that's exactly what I did. The players were larger than life, and the atmosphere was electric. And then, it happened—I actually caught a ball! I couldn't believe it. My heart raced as I clutched it, grinning from ear to ear. I even managed to get a few autographs from some of the players, who were just as friendly as they were famous.

For the longest time, that day was the best day of my life. My mom, who was usually so strict about school, had taken me out of class to surprise me with something beyond my wildest dreams. The fact that she did something so out of character made it even more special.

On the drive home, I was exhausted, my head spinning with excitement.

My friends couldn't believe it the next day at school when I told them what had happened. Most were jealous, and a few didn't even believe me. But I didn't care. I had the memories, the ball, and the autographs. I always hoped for future "dentist appointments," but it never happened again. But it's ok—I have this perfect memory to cherish to this day.

Memory Prompts

- Did you ever play hooky at school? If so, share your experience(s).

- Was there ever a time when you got to skip school for something fun because of your parents? What did you do, and how did it feel?

- If you could meet any sports hero back in the day, who would it be?

Chapter 35

Passover Delight

Passover was my mother's favorite holiday. It was the one time of year when the woman who claimed to hate cooking would transform into a culinary genius. The kitchen, usually a place of quick meals and simple fare, became a hub of activity, filled with the sounds and smells of tradition.

I remember waking up on Passover morning, filled with joy not only because I got to stay home from school but also because of what awaited me downstairs. The first thing that would hit me as I descended the stairs was the warm, glorious smell of brisket slow-cooking in ancient electric cookers. These cookers were dusted off and brought out every year for this special occasion, and they held within them the essence of my mother's secret Passover recipe.

This wasn't your typical barbecue brisket. My mother's version was a rich, savory masterpiece, made slowly with fresh tomatoes, celery, carrots, and onions, all perfectly seasoned with her "secret Passover" mix of spices. I'd sneak a taste whenever I could. It was a flavor that, to this day, nothing else quite compares to.

A pot of chicken soup would be simmering on the stove, its golden broth shimmering as my mother carefully skimmed the fat from the surface. Every kid thinks their mother makes the best chicken soup, but my mother's truly was something special. Guests wise enough to visit on Passover would ask for second and third helpings, even though they knew a huge meal was still to come. Her matzoh balls were always perfectly fluffy and light; my father would joke that they were "a true feat of engineering."

As my mother peeled apples for the kugel, she would hum softly to herself, a content smile on her face. The kugel was sweet yet slightly savory, a dish that seemed to get better as the days went by. We'd enjoy it cold for the next week, its flavors deepening with time. Inevitably, my mother would slip a piece into my lunchbox alongside a peanut butter and jelly sandwich made with matzoh instead of bread. It was her way of extending the holiday, of keeping that Passover magic alive just a little longer.

The only thing my mother didn't make from scratch was the infamous gefilte fish. She'd buy it in jars, and as a child, I couldn't stand the sight of her scraping the jelly off those cold fish cakes. But somehow, I'd eat it doused in bright pink horseradish every year.

Passover food will always hold a special place in my heart. I doubt I'll ever taste anything as good as those Passover meals from my childhood. But every year, as I prepare for the holiday, I find myself trying to recreate a bit of that magic, hoping to pass it on to my own family, just as my mother did for me.

Memory Prompts

- Do you have a memory of helping out in the kitchen during the holidays or a special occasion? What role did you play?

- Have you ever tried to recreate a family recipe? How did it turn out?

- Was there a family recipe or dish you didn't like but had to eat because it was a tradition growing up?

Chapter 36

My 70s Toys

The toys of the 1970s seem so simple compared to today's gadgets, yet they brought so much joy.

My favorite toy, without a doubt, was my Stingray bike. It was a sleek, shiny thing with a banana seat and high-rise handlebars that made me feel like I was riding a chopper straight out of a movie. I spent hours zipping up and down the neighborhood, the wind in my hair, convinced I was the fastest kid on the block. That bike was my ticket to freedom, and it took me on countless adventures, from daring races with friends to leisurely rides that let my imagination run wild.

Another toy that holds a special place in my heart was the bottle cutter kit I got one Christmas. It seemed like such a simple concept—cutting glass bottles to turn them into drinking glasses, vases, or whatever else my mind could conjure up. But to me, it was a way to create something with my own hands. I'd gather up old soda bottles and carefully score them with the cutter, holding my breath as I hoped for a clean break.

Then there was the Wham-O's Water Wiggle, a toy as unpredictable as it was fun. You'd hook it up to the garden hose, and it would whip around wildly, spraying water everywhere. It was the perfect way to cool off on a hot summer day.

And no trip down memory lane would be complete without mentioning the infamous lawn darts. It's hard to believe now that we played with something potentially dangerous, but back then, it was all good fun. We'd stand at opposite ends of the yard, aiming those heavy, metal-tipped darts at plastic rings on the grass.

Stretch Armstrong was another staple of my toy collection, with his impossibly stretchy limbs that we'd pull and twist in every direction. He was practically indestructible—or so we thought until we finally stretched him one too many times.

I also spent countless hours with my Spirograph, creating intricate patterns that felt like works of art. I'd sit at the kitchen table, carefully placing the colored pens in the gears, watching in awe as the designs took shape on the paper. It was mesmerizing, and it never got old, no matter how many times I did it.

And who could forget the clackers? We'd swing those noisy, plastic balls on strings up and down, trying to get them to click together just right. My trainer roller skates, with their metal wheels, rounded out my collection of favorite toys. I'd strap them on and glide down the sidewalk, the wheels clattering against the concrete, feeling like I was flying. There was nothing quite like the sense of speed and freedom they gave me.

In a world without screens or smartphones, those toys were all we needed to create memories that would last a lifetime.

Memory Prompts

- What was your favorite childhood toy, and what made it so special to you?

- How do you think toys these days compare to those you played with growing up?

- Did you ever drink from the hose growing up?

Chapter 37

Mini Bikes

When I was a kid, I had a Honda CT-70 minibike, a group of friends who had their own wheels, and miles upon miles of dirt roads and backwoods to explore. Every morning during the summer, I'd kick-start my minibike, feeling the rumble of the engine beneath me as I set out to meet my friends. We'd take off down those dusty roads, the wind in our hair, the sun on our backs, with no real destination in mind.

The tank on my bike held exactly 24 cents worth of gas, enough to carry me through an entire day of adventure. We'd wind our way through the woods, racing each other on the narrow trails, dodging low-hanging branches, and laughing whenever someone took a turn too fast and ended up in the bushes. There was nothing like flying down those dirt roads, the roar of the minibike in my ears, and the knowledge that the day was ours to shape however we wanted.

When the sun hung high in the sky, and our stomachs started to grumble, we'd head into town, our bikes kicking up clouds of dust as we approached the one café that sat under the town's single blinking traffic light. We'd park our bikes out front, the engines still hot and ticking as they cooled down, and head inside for a well-deserved break.

The café was our little haven—a place where we could relax, joke around, and refuel for the next leg of our journey. We'd order cokes and french fries, the kind that was perfectly crisp and golden, and shoot pool in the back room, the clack of the balls and the hum of the jukebox filling the air.

Our parents didn't worry about us back then. They knew we'd be out all day and that we'd come home when the sun set, our faces dirty, our clothes dusty, and our hearts full. There was a sense of trust and freedom that's hard to imagine now, but it was just the way things were.

Now, when I visit my hometown, it's hard to believe it's the same place that once held so much thrill for me. The roads are still there, and the café still sits under the blinking light, but it all feels smaller somehow, like a forgotten piece of a puzzle I used to know so well. It's as if the thrill was never in the town itself but in the way we saw it, through the eyes of kids who believed the world was ours to conquer.

Memory Prompts

- Was there a group of friends you spent your childhood exploring or adventuring with? What were some of your favorite memories with them?

- Is there a place from your childhood that feels different to you now? How has your perspective on it changed over the years?

- What simple pleasures from your youth do you miss the most?

Chapter 38

Days at the Ballpark

For me, summer mornings in the 1970s meant one thing: baseball.

I'd roll out of bed and quickly pack up my ball glove, stuffing as many baseballs as I could into the pockets of my old backpack. My bat was too long to fit, so I'd slide it through the handles of my bike, a trusty companion that had seen more than its fair share of dirt roads and ballpark trips.

The ride to the ballpark was always the start of the adventure. My friends and I would meet along the way, our bikes weaving through the neighborhood streets, the sound of laughter and the occasional squeak of a rusty chain filling the air.

We'd play pickup baseball for hours, the rules as loose as our imaginations allowed. Sometimes, we had enough kids for two full teams; other times, we'd make do with just a handful of players, taking turns at bat, chasing down fly balls, and arguing over whether a pitch was a strike or a ball. There was no umpire to call the shots, just the group's collective decision, and somehow, it always worked out.

We'd dive for grounders, slide into home plate, and race around the bases until our legs felt like jelly. The sun climbed higher, beating down on us, but we barely noticed.

After six or seven hours of nonstop action, hunger would finally force us to take a break. I'd ride home, tired but happy, grab whatever was in the fridge—usually a peanut butter and jelly sandwich or leftover pizza—and wolf it down. But the day wasn't over yet. There was still the "real game" to be played.

I'd change into my little league uniform, which made me feel like a pro, even if it was a bit too big and the socks never quite stayed up. Then it was back to the ballpark for the official game, with coaches, parents, and a scoreboard keeping track of every run, hit, and out.

The game was serious business, but it was also the highlight of the day. The cheers from the stands, the thrill of stepping up to the plate, and the sense of pride in being part of a team made those summer evenings so special.

If we were lucky, we'd get a Shasta soda and a bag of chips from the concession stand after the game. And if we were really lucky, the whole team would head to the A&W for dinner, piling into cars with our parents, our uniforms still dusty from the game.

We'd sit at the long tables, laughing and reliving the game. The taste of burgers and root beer floats made those baseball days feel just a little more perfect.

Memory Prompts

- Baseball seemed to be a big pasttime for many of these stories. Was baseball popular for you growing up, or was there another sport or activity that was just as popular?

- Do you recall a time when you felt completely carefree, with the whole day ahead of you to do as you pleased? What did you do with that time?

- Were you close to the kids in your neighborhood when you were young?

Passing the Magic Along

Thank you so much for reading my book. I hope you've enjoyed strolling down memory lane with these short stories. Your honest opinion on Amazon is not just a review; it would serve as a beacon for other seniors, caregivers, and family members, guiding them to the stories they're looking for and helping to pass the nostalgia, stimulation, and connection forward.

Simply click here or scan the QR code below to leave your review:

The joy of reminiscing and storytelling is kept alive when we pass on our experiences – and you're helping to do just that.

Sincerely,

Lillian Whitmore
info@seniorshortstories.com

www.ingramcontent.com/pod-product-compliance
Lightning Source LLC
Chambersburg PA
CBHW08081725O626
47159CB00010B/3412